A WHALE'S TALE
FROM THE SUPPER SEA

BY C.J. AND BA REA

BAS RELIEF PUBLISHING GROUP • GLENSHAW, PA

Dedicated
to our children
Madeleine Rea,
Mindy King and Jason King
because they are the
reason for the journey.
And to our friends
Bob Satin
and
Bill Schiff
who have helped us
along the way.

Dear Readers,

We hope you will enjoy exploring the Supper Sea. You will meet some fascinating animals while you and Alice look for her friend Meg.

The Minstrel Krill will sing *Meg's Song* on the bottom of each page for the young and young at heart.

Be sure to stop along the way to read between the pages. You'll find lots of information about humpback whales.

C. J. and Ba

Text © C.J. and Ba Rea 1999
Illustrations © Ba Rea 1999
All rights reserved
Published by
Bas Relief Publishing Group, P.O. Box 426, Glenshaw, PA 15116
Printed by Schiff Printing Inc., Pittsburgh, PA

ISBN 0-9657472-1-2
Library of Congress Catalog Card Number 98-93836

Alice sat outside the entrance to her burrow.

"Where is she? Where is she?" the tufted puffin muttered. "The water is calm. The sky is clear. I ought to be able to spot her, somewhere."

In the five seasons they had known each other, Meg had always returned to the Supper Sea first. As Alice worried from her sky-high perch, she remembered the day she had met her best friend in a huge school of krill. Meg's voice had surrounded her.

Who ever heard of a krill playing guitar?

Let me tell you a tale that we sing in the kelp.
If you wonder about humpbacks then *Meg's Song* will help.

It starts high on an island in the great Supper Sea,
Where Alice, the puffin, was as worried as could be.

You see her friend Meg had been gone for so long,
Poor Alice thought something just might have gone wrong.

You notice she never says. "Excuse me. I just swallowed your entire family line."

Alice met Meg in a big school of krill.
She barely escaped being part of Meg's meal.

"Eating birds makes me choke. Alice, you needn't worry.
I don't want my food to be feathered or furry."

"I'm glad to hear that," Alice said with a sigh.
"For more krill let's give Wavy Kelp Bay a try."

CAREFUL SWALLOWED YOU!

A large gray shadow next to Alice began to move.

"DON'T BE AFRAID."

"Afraid? Me? Hardly. I just get my feathers a little ruffled when an island with an appetite tries to have me for lunch."

"I won't hurt you. Mom told me I shouldn't eat birds. She said I'd gag on anything larger than a murrelet."

"I'm so relieved to hear that," said Alice.

"What's your name?" asked the whale.

"I'm Alice Cirrhata."

"My name's Meg Novaengliae."

"Nice to meet you Meg but you've done a very good job of scaring away my krill. I need to go find lunch."

"I'm sorry. Let me help you," said the whale.

"OK," said Alice. "Do you know Wavy Kelp Bay? It's off of Big Bay, three bays up from the loud place on the side where the sun rises."

"I know the one," said Meg.

"It's a quick flight. I'll meet you there." Alice took off, thinking she might have time for a bite of something before the humpback arrived.

The humpback whale, *Megaptera novaengliae*, is a large marine mammal. It can reach 52 feet in length and weigh 50 tons.

Our name, "Krill," comes from a Norwegian word for creepy-crawly things.

The North Pacific humpback spends its summers feeding in rich northern waters. It eats small fish such as herring, capelin and sandlance and even smaller, shrimp-like creatures known as krill. The humpback is one of the 11 types of mysticete whales. Mysticete means "mustached," and describes the special hair-lined plates that these whales use to strain food from the water.

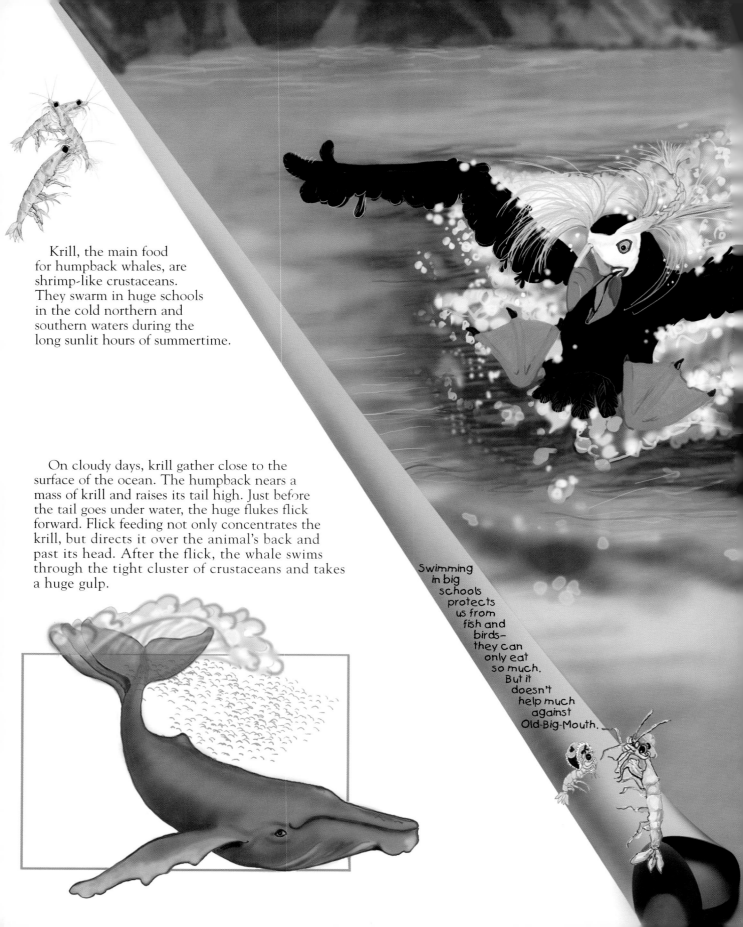

Krill, the main food for humpback whales, are shrimp-like crustaceans. They swarm in huge schools in the cold northern and southern waters during the long sunlit hours of summertime.

On cloudy days, krill gather close to the surface of the ocean. The humpback nears a mass of krill and raises its tail high. Just before the tail goes under water, the huge flukes flick forward. Flick feeding not only concentrates the krill, but directs it over the animal's back and past its head. After the flick, the whale swims through the tight cluster of crustaceans and takes a huge gulp.

Swimming in big schools protects us from fish and birds— they can only eat so much. But it doesn't help much against Old-Big-Mouth.

As she landed in the quiet bay, Alice was startled by a fountain of mist followed immediately by a humpback whale.

"Watch this!" Alice heard Meg say.

The whale created a wave with her flukes that sent Alice flying through the air without the help of her wings. When she landed, the puffin saw krill lying still in the water all around her.

"What did you do to these krill?" she asked.

Meg's mouth was full and it took her a minute to answer. "Oh, it's just a little trick I use. The krill will never know what ate 'em," she said after a big swallow.

At the bay, Meg showed Alice a very fine trick. With her tail fluke she made a really loud flick.

Alice went flying, not using her wings. She landed to find out what flick fishing brings.

All around them the water was covered with krill. "It's dinner!" said Alice. "Oh Meg, this is swell!"

From that very day they have been best of friends.
They always feel sad when the feasting time ends.

Last year Meg had eaten like a whale and a half.
She told her friend Alice she would soon have a calf.

She had to eat fish and krill by the ton,
'Cause there wouldn't be food in the hot southern sun.

Ever think
about moving south?

From that day on, Alice and Meg had been friends. Each year, Meg was waiting for Alice when she returned to the Supper Sea in the spring. In late summer, when Alice's puffling fledged, Meg always followed it to see that it made its way safely out to the Deep Blue Sea.

Last year Meg had been unusually hungry.

"Hey, if you swallow the whole bay we'll have to learn to walk," joked Alice, who now knew the advantage of having a 40-ton friend to knock her meal unconscious.

"I'll put the water back," gargled Meg. "It's just the fish and krill I need. Did I mention I'm pregnant?"

"So you're fishing for two?" asked Alice.

"Oh, it's much worse than that. It's more like I'm fishing for four. When I leave the Supper Sea I don't get to eat again until I return next spring with a 15-ton calf. And guess whose blubber feeds those 15 tons?"

"Yikes, and I thought catching an extra 14 fish a day for my puffling was a workout," said Alice.

When Meg left to head south she had waved her usual, "See you next year!"

By late September there isn't nearly as much light here in the Supper Sea. So its slim pickings for the krill as well.

Humpback whales live in all of the oceans of the world. North Pacific humpbacks come to Alaska in the late spring to feed. By late September the food supply runs low. Then the whales leave for the warmer waters of Hawaii. The pregnant females are the last to leave the feeding grounds. It is important that they have enough blubber to see them through the winter months of giving birth and nursing in the tropical waters.

Meg had told Alice that all Supper Sea humpbacks went to Hawaii each year. The male humpbacks would sing beautiful songs to the females. The female humpbacks would tend to their newborn calves. Then, when the calves were ready, they'd make the journey back to the Supper Sea. Alice was sure she had heard Meg say they always returned, but she had been watching for her friend for nearly two weeks.

It takes the humpbacks of Kenai Fjords, Alaska, more than two months to make the journey south.

In Hawaii, the males will sing beautiful songs, which researchers believe are used to attract a mate.

Ultimately, the female whale and her calf of the previous season are joined by a male. The male swims behind them, protecting his potential mate from other suitors. Pregnant females find a quiet spot away from the mating animals to give birth to their young.

Calves are born tail first. Often another female humpback will attend the birth. Soon after birth, the calf must be nudged gently to the surface for its first breath of air.

The mothers and their newborn calves will be the last to leave Hawaii. The calves must build up enough fat from nursing to keep themselves warm on the feeding grounds.

Our eggs sink to deep water where krill babies are safe from the Ocean-Swallowers until their yolk-sacs run out.

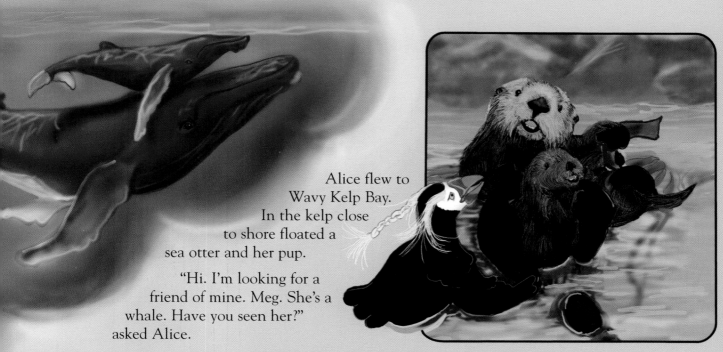

Alice flew to
Wavy Kelp Bay.
In the kelp close
to shore floated a
sea otter and her pup.

"Hi. I'm looking for a
friend of mine. Meg. She's a
whale. Have you seen her?"
asked Alice.

"We get a lot of whales, but not all at once; the bay's too small. What's she look like?"

"Well, she's long and she has a great big mouth and a sizable tail and she..."

"Wait a minute," interrupted the otter, "you swim, don't you?"

"Of course."

"I've been working on this problem recently. Follow me."

In Hawaii's warm waters Meg would bask in the sun.
With all of her whale friends, she'd have lots of fun.

In the spring she'd give birth to her very first calf.
"Meg with a baby?" That made Alice laugh.

But now it WAS spring. Meg was late coming back.
Alice watched from the rookery for two weeks, in fact.

What if Meg couldn't eat? What if something had got her?
Alice flew off to see Luty the otter.

The otter led Alice under water to a small cave. She pointed to a pile of rocks. There was a carved rock for nearly every creature in the Supper Sea.

"Where did these come from?" asked Alice in amazement.

"Utensils. I use them to crack open crabs and mussels, anything with a shell. I like to carve as I eat. Here, look at these three, I just started whales. A killer whale, a fin whale..."

"It's Meg!" Alice shouted as the otter handed her one of the rocks. "She's a humpback." Alice turned it over and over. "It even has her fluke markings!"

"Oh yes. She fed in the bay a lot last summer," said the otter.

"But what's this?" asked Alice, pointing to a small mark.

"That's my name, 'Luty,'" said the otter. "Why don't you take that with you? I haven't seen Meg this season but other animals might recognize her."

"Oh Luty, thank you. May you find the perfect feathers for your nest," said Alice.

"You're welcome," said Luty, wondering what she would ever do with a nest or feathers.

Humpback Whale

Fin Whale

Minke Whale

For some reason human's call the Orca a "Killer Whale." But in our family, we think of the humpback as the Killer Whale.

There are many mammals that live in the ocean. Those belonging to the Order Cetacea have adapted to a completely aquatic existence. There are two types of cetaceans. The Odonteceti are cetaceans with teeth. Those that strain their food from the water with baleen are called Mysticeti. Several species of both types of cetaceans spend time feeding in the Kenai Fjords during the summer. Among the Odonteceti are the orca whales, harbor porpoise and dall's porpoise. The baleen users are the fin whale, the humpback whale, and the minke whale.

Orca Whale

Dall's Porpoise

Harbour Porpoise

The otter made pictures in rocks when she ate.
For opening mussels and crabs, they were great.

One rock looked like Meg; it was shaped like the whale.
"Alice, you take it. Tell the others your tale.

'Cause so far this year, I haven't seen Meg."
Said Luty, "I'd never miss something so big."

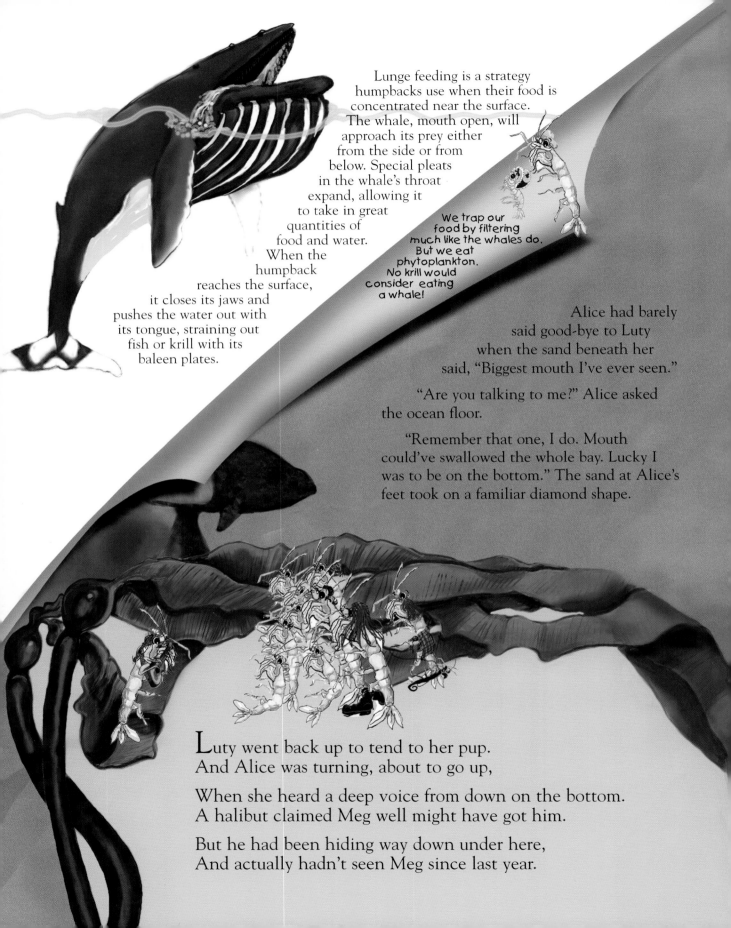

Lunge feeding is a strategy humpbacks use when their food is concentrated near the surface. The whale, mouth open, will approach its prey either from the side or from below. Special pleats in the whale's throat expand, allowing it to take in great quantities of food and water. When the humpback reaches the surface, it closes its jaws and pushes the water out with its tongue, straining out fish or krill with its baleen plates.

We trap our food by filtering much like the whales do. But we eat phytoplankton. No krill would consider eating a whale!

Alice had barely said good-bye to Luty when the sand beneath her said, "Biggest mouth I've ever seen."

"Are you talking to me?" Alice asked the ocean floor.

"Remember that one, I do. Mouth could've swallowed the whole bay. Lucky I was to be on the bottom." The sand at Alice's feet took on a familiar diamond shape.

Luty went back up to tend to her pup.
And Alice was turning, about to go up,

When she heard a deep voice from down on the bottom.
A halibut claimed Meg well might have got him.

But he had been hiding way down under here,
And actually hadn't seen Meg since last year.

"Halibut!" said Alice.

"Puffin," said the fish.

"You've seen Meg?"

"Watched it all from down here. Marathon eating machine. That mouth just kept growing. Took in 18 generations of krill at once."

"When? Which way did she go? Did she have a calf with her?"

"Last year. South. Hawaii maybe. I didn't see a calf."

"Oh, last year..." Alice sighed.

Alice left the halibut and flew to a nearby island. Mr. and Mrs. Oystercatcher were dining on a meal of fresh mussels. "Yoo-hoo, Ms. Puffin. Would you care to join us for lunch?" they called out.

Alice, not sure how one ate mussels, replied, "I've just eaten, but perhaps we could talk while you have your lunch."

"I didn't know puffins were in the habit of carrying luggage," said Mr. Oystercatcher pointing to the carving of Meg.

"Luty, the otter, sculpted this to look like a friend of mine. Her name is Meg," explained Alice. "She's lost. Have you seen her?"

"Look, it's Backwards," he said.

"Well I can turn her around for you," said Alice.

"No, dear," said Mrs. Oystercatcher. "What he means is she's the whale we call 'Backwards' because her dorsal fin makes her look like she's going backwards. I haven't seen her this year. But she was always here in the evenings last year."

Seeing the worried look on Alice's face she added, "Oh don't worry, dear, those humpbacks always return. No other animal depends so much on the Supper Sea for its food."

The Oystercatcher's words did not help. Now Alice was worried that Meg might be very hungry. "I should be going now; there are so many places to look. If you see Meg, please send word. I live on the seaward side of the rookery overlooking the Roaring Beach."

The Oystercatchers waved good-bye as
Alice flew toward Pile of Rocks Island.

On Oystercatcher Island, two mussel-eating black birds
Remembered our Meg as the whale they called "Backwards."

They hadn't seen Meg since late the last fall.
She was feeding non-stop and round as a ball.

The birds said, "Don't worry, Meg will come back to eat.
There aren't any fish for her down in that heat."

Alice said, "Thank you," and left in a hurry.
"Poor Meg needs this food," Alice started to worry.

Always be careful around a humpback. If it dives, it is bound to show up back at the surface with its mouth wide open!

The common name, "humpback," describes the arch of the whale's back just before it makes a deep dive. The dorsal fin sits at the top of the arch, drawing even more attention to the "hump" of whale sticking out of the water. The dorsal fin is very small and sickle shaped. Because it is loaded with blood vessels and has no insulating blubber, it may be used to help the whale cool off.

Pile of Rocks was a place Alice liked to go to think. It was a very small island looking out on the Gulf of Alaska and rarely used by other animals.

"Excuse me, excuse me, the tide's coming in. More to the point, you're standing on my limbs, and if you don't move I will not be able to eat!"

"Oh my! My apologies, I didn't notice you down there," said Alice to what appeared to be a rather irritated barnacle.

"If YOU had YOUR head glued to a rock, YOU would notice a lot more of what goes on around you. As it is, you're lucky to have a head at all, waving it around in the air, no plates to protect it. It's a wonder you don't get it bitten right off," spat the barnacle.

"I've always thought my head quite safe, though I worry about my feet sometimes," said Alice.

"Quit stomping around on beds of barnacles with them and we'd all be a lot safer. Oh I wish I had been a whale rider like my second cousin Corny. He gets to ride through the richest clouds of zooplankton. Never gets stepped on," said the barnacle.

"Corny?"

"Short for Coronula. Rides with a humpback named Meg," the barnacle said.

"Meg? Have you seen her?"

"No, come to think of it, Corny hasn't been by since last fall." With that, the barnacle began waving his cirri to the incoming tide and ignored Alice.

Holding onto the whale is one good way to avoid getting swallowed by it!

Certain parasites make their homes on humpback whales. Barnacles attach themselves to the flukes, flippers, chin, and ventral pleats of the whales. They feed, like the whale, by filtering zooplankton out of the water. Barnacles settle on the whales in the northern latitudes, often contributing an additional 1000 pounds to a whale's weight. However, they tend to fall off in the tropical waters.

Whale lice are even less pleasant visitors. They feed on diatoms and other material found on the whales' skin. They have specially designed legs with pincers to hold on to the whale.

On Pile of Rocks Island Alice had hoped to think
But an angry old barnacle put up a stink.

By mistake, on his shell, poor Alice had stood.
And he let her know that it just was no good.

His cousin had settled on Meg's right-hand fin,
But it had been months since he'd heard from him.

He'd really seen nothing, his head stuck to that rock;
He was eating right now and did not want to talk.

Alice could see a large crowd of birds gathering on the water by the entrance to Big Bay. She flew in to join them for what was surely a feast of fish under the waves.

Once her belly was full, Alice swam to the surface, popping out of the water in the middle of 500 kittiwakes.

"Great fishing today!" said 50 of the birds to Alice. The kittiwakes were always polite, but they all talked at once. It was a little bit confusing. Alice couldn't remember ever talking to just one kittiwake.

"Yup, nothing like a school of sandlance," said Alice. She took the sculpture of Meg out from under her wing.

"What's that?" asked the 20 kittiwakes nearest Alice.

Alice heard kittiwakes and she had a hunch
If she flew to their noise she'd find that day's lunch.

After lunch underwater, she returned to the surface
Smack dab in the middle of a kittiwake circus.

Those birds had seen whales rounding fish up for snacks
There'd been three Hairy-Bubble-Blowers—
    the birds' name for humpbacks.

With a flap of her wings, Alice took off again.
She'd check Roaring Beach in search of her friend.

"It's a carving of my friend Meg. She's a humpback whale. She lives here in the summer, but I haven't seen her this year," said Alice.

"Oh, a Hairy-Bubble-Blower," said a group of kittiwakes to her left.

"What?" asked Alice.

"That's just what we call them. They come up sometimes right where we're feeding. Their mouths are wide open, and they're all hairy inside," said a group to her right. "And those bubbles they make! Felt like we were in a boiling ocean this morning at Roaring Beach."

"There were Hairy-Bubble-Blowers, I mean humpback whales, at Roaring Beach today?" Alice asked excitedly.

"Two or three of 'em," said eight or ten kittiwakes.

"I need to go see if Meg is home," said Alice, tucking the carving into her feathers again. "Good fishing to you."

"See you soon!" called 500 kittiwakes.

WARNING.
The information between these pages is graphic in nature and may not be suitable for young krill.

The roof of a humpback's open mouth looks hairy.

The coarse fibrous hairs are connected to 250-400 pairs of baleen plates.

Humpback whales sometimes make bubble nets to trap their food. Swimming in a tight circle, they release bubbles from their blow holes at regular intervals. The bubbles surround and confuse their prey. They can make the net very wide at the surface, accommodating several whales, or as small as 15 feet across for one whale. Bubble size (net mesh) can also be varied depending on prey size. Then the whales swim through the concentration of fish or krill, filling their tremendous mouths.

Researchers identify individual humpback whales by the black and white pattern on the bottom of the whale's tail. These fluke markings are as unique as fingerprints are for people. Many whales also have scrapes or portions of their flukes missing.

About 25 years ago, scientists started to put together a photo catalogue to identify individual whales. The humpbacks help by waving "good-bye" with their flukes every time they make a deep dive.

To krill, all humpbacks are the same ...bad news!

As she flew above the Roaring Beach, Alice saw no sign of whales. She flew past the big, ill-tempered, bull sea lions who gave the place its name. Far down the beach on a large rock, five young male sea lions sprawled in the mid-day sun. Alice landed near them, knowing they would be much friendlier than the older bulls on the main beach.

"AH HEM. Good morning," said Alice. The nearest sea lion lifted his head. Another opened his eyes, shielding them from the sun with a long fore flipper. A third rolled over and covered his ears. The last two did not stir.

"We don't get many puffins on our rock," said the first sea lion.

"The racket your fathers make does not sound like a welcome call," said Alice.

"Yeah, you're right. That's why we don't spend much time on their beach."

"Were any of you awake this morning when the humpbacks were fishing off your beach?" asked Alice.

"I wasn't awake until they were fishing off our beach," said the second sea lion.

"Did one of them look like this?" asked Alice as she pulled out the carving of Meg.

"Hey, I remember that whale," said one of the sea lions. "I'd never seen a fluke marking like that before. She was here a lot last year. Fed 'round the clock it seemed."

"Everyone saw her last year, but no one's seen her this season," sighed Alice.

"You should ask the dall's porpoise. They travel all over the Supper Sea. They're bound to see all of the creatures living here," said one sea lion.

"Thanks for the tip," said Alice. "I hope I can find them. Those porpoise move like they're late for tomorrow's lunch."

At the beach five young sea lions slept away from the crowd.
Alice didn't go close to the bulls who were loud.

They'd all heard the whales feeding early that day,
But Meg hadn't been there. That much they could say.

"The dall's porpoise travel the whole Supper Sea.
Why don't you ask them where your friend Meg might be?"

Alice flew high above the Supper Sea looking for the telltale waves made by porpoise fins cutting the water at top speeds. Off in the distance, close to the head of Peopled Bay, she saw them. It was a long flight. Alice hoped she could catch them.

As she drew close, she spotted the porpoise playing in the bow wake of a sailboat. The puffin, struggling to catch up to the boat, landed on its bow. Breathing heavily, Alice tried to get the attention of the animals in the water beneath her.

"Hallo, down there!" Alice yelled. The porpoise swam back and forth under the bow, enjoying themselves, not even noticing Alice. Then the puffin had an idea. She pulled out the carving of Meg and heaved it into the water, careful not to hit the animals.

A moment later one porpoise surfaced briefly, "Did you drop this?" he asked, tossing the sculpture to Alice. He fell back into the water as the other porpoise came up on the other side.

"Yes," said Alice to the second animal. "I hope I didn't hit you." This is harder than talking to kittiwakes, thought Alice.

"No, you missed us. Hey, is that a sculpture of Meg *Novaengliae?*" asked the first porpoise as it dove back under.

"Yes," said Alice to the second porpoise as it glided out of the water. "Have you seen her?"

"Not since last year," said the porpoise disappearing underwater.

Alice found two dall's porpoise swimming in Peopled Bay.
From the bow of a boat she could hear what they'd say.

She dropped the rock shaped like Meg in the water.
The porpoise said "Hallo, you dropped this, we caught her."

"It's Meg! Have we seen her? Not for many a day.
Though last year we frolicked all through Green Soup Bay."

"Ask the terns if they've seen her. They'd have the best chance.
That long-distance travel is part of their dance."

"We played in Green Soup Bay with our two-holed cousin several times last fall before she left," said the other porpoise as it surfaced.

"Oh dear," said Alice. "No one's seen her this year. I hope she's all right."

"Talk to the arctic terns; they travel south like Meg," said one porpoise with a splash.

"They might have seen her," shouted the other. "Good luck!" And with that, both porpoise sped off down the bay and out of sight.

Now there's a view of that whale that you won't see back home.

One of the main differences between the baleen whales and the toothed whales is the blowhole. Toothed whales have just one blowhole, but baleen whales have two. The "blow" of the humpback whale can be 6 to 20 feet high. When you see the blow of any cetacean, you are actually seeing water vapor. The warm air expelled from the animal's lungs expands and the water vapor in it condenses creating a white plume.

The terns nested at the head of Peopled Bay. Alice called out to a group of them circling over the boats in the People's Marina. Calling back in their high-pitched voices they landed around her on the jetty.

"Oh, poor dear, you look tired. What brings you to Peopled Bay?" asked the first tern to arrive. "I thought you puffins preferred the rocky cliffs and islands."

As the rest of the terns landed, Alice told them the story of Meg.

"So you see, I am very worried. My friend needs to be eating by now. Her blubber is surely running out. She can't make it much longer without the Supper Sea." Alice's voice was tired and sad.

"I might have seen your friend," said a young tern. "I got lost one day in some heavy fog. When I could finally see again I wasn't sure where I was. Then I saw three humpback whales ahead of me—a mother and two calves. We all come to the Supper Sea each spring so I knew I was still on course. I did think it was a little odd that they were still traveling. The humpbacks usually get here before we do. If that was your friend, I bet she will be here any day now.

I think they are following us!

Krill breeding grounds

Krill breeding grounds

HUMPBACK WHALE MIGRATION

▮ Migration route
◖ Breeding grounds
▮ Summer Feeding grounds

Populations of the arctic tern and the humpback whale can be found all over our planet from north to south because of their migration patterns. Humpbacks from both hemispheres feed near the poles in the summer and migrate to the equator to breed in the winter. The arctic tern breeds in the Arctic summer, and then travels all the way to the Antarctic for the rest of the year, accomplishing worldwide distribution strictly through migration.

"Oh my, this is very good news! Thank you so much. I should go home now so I'll be ready when she gets here!" said Alice.

"Now wait just a minute, young puffin!" an older tern spoke up. "I may not be a puffin, but I know an exhausted bird when I see one. No use flying to meet your friend until you have enough strength to get where you're going. Tonight you'll sleep there." The tern pointed to an enormous cruise ship just behind them.

"But that's a peopled ship," said Alice.

"I know. It's a peopled ship that will pull out of here at four in the morning. By the time the people begin to stir, you'll have cruised as far as Oystercatcher Island. You'll get a good rest, an easy ride back home, and your wings won't fall off from the strain. You puffins are great swimmers, but you should stick to short-distance flights."

Alice knew the tern was right. She had been so worried about Meg that she had flown too far. She waited on the jetty until midnight. The big ship was quiet when she settled in to get some sleep.

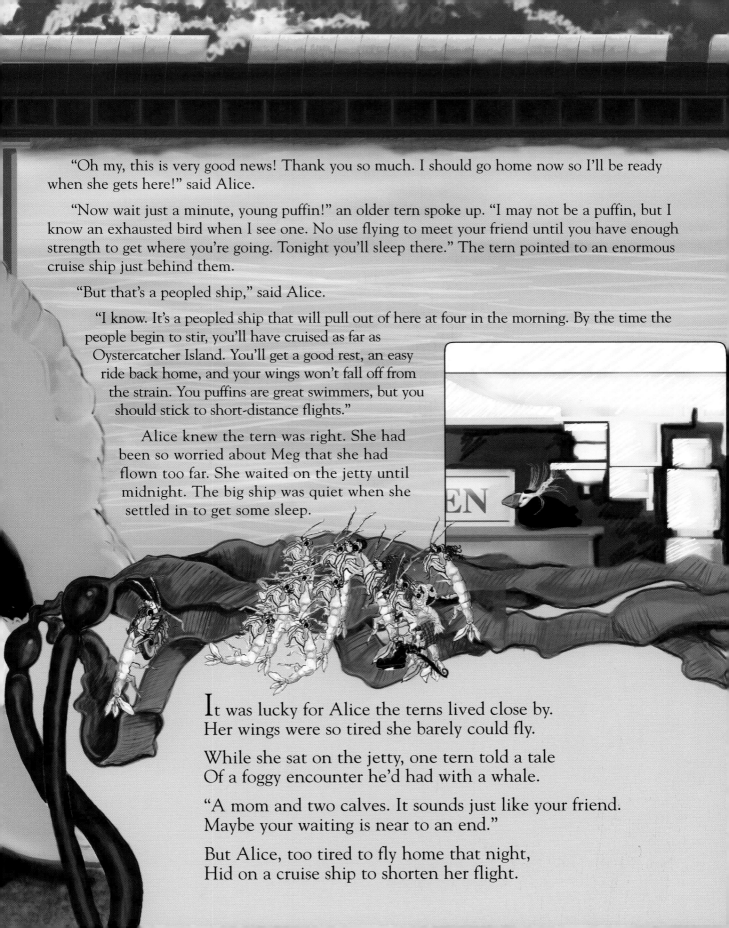

It was lucky for Alice the terns lived close by.
Her wings were so tired she barely could fly.

While she sat on the jetty, one tern told a tale
Of a foggy encounter he'd had with a whale.

"A mom and two calves. It sounds just like your friend.
Maybe your waiting is near to an end."

But Alice, too tired to fly home that night,
Hid on a cruise ship to shorten her flight.

Alice woke as Oystercatcher Island was coming into view. She stayed on the boat a little longer to get as close as she could to Green Soup Bay, where the porpoise had played with Meg last year. The land around the bay rose swiftly. She could get a good view of the entrance to the Supper Sea. When the big ship turned out toward the Deep Blue Sea, Alice flew up to a rocky outcropping and scanned the water for Meg.

"No sign of her," sighed Alice aloud, wondering if that tern had really seen them at all.

"Who is SHE-EE-EE?" bleated a rather deep, yet friendly, voice.

Alice turned around to see a large, nanny mountain goat. "Oh, good morning. I didn't notice you," said Alice, surprised.

She flew to a cliff from the big, peopled boat.
High above the green water she met Nanny Goat.

The goats' twins were jumping just above reach,
Where they were the first to see Meg's twins breach.

They were jumping and cheering for this was the end.
Now Alice, the puffin, could go see her friend.

"I just got here," said Nanny Goat, pointing to an impossibly steep rock where two kid goats were scrambling to join them. "It is a fine spot for viewing what the day has to bring. Don't you think?"

"I'm hoping the day brings my friend Meg and her two new calves," said Alice.

"Meg Novaengliae?" asked the goat.

"You know her?" Alice asked excitedly.

"Well, she was here nearly every day last year. Always feeding. If she had two calves that would certainly explain her appetite. It takes a lot more of everything to raise two." The goat glanced over at her kids jumping around on the rocks.

"I've never had two," said Alice.

Just then the twin kid goats began to jump up and down. It made Alice nervous to see youngsters this high up with no wings to help them if they slipped.

"Mama, mama!" they shouted together.

"Oh look!" said Nanny Goat. Over by Beehive Two, splashing filled the water. Alice's heart leapt as she saw an enormous splash followed by two slightly smaller walls of water shooting skyward.

"It's Meg! It's Meg! She's back!" cried Alice. She was so excited she jumped even higher than the kids. Then, with one huge jump, she was off. Flapping as fast as she could, she flew to meet her friend.

Pikers! In one summer a female krill will release 20,000 eggs and WE fend for ourselves from the day we hatch!

Most of the animals in our story have just one baby at a time. Sometimes they have only one every two or three years. Mammals give birth to babies that are not prepared to live on their own. This means the parents, often the female parent alone, must be able to provide for themselves and their young. Twins do not always survive because the mother can not provide enough for two. When a humpback whale gives birth to twins, they are much smaller than single baby humpbacks.

Alice landed on a rock as close as she could get to the three breaching whales.

"There you are!" boomed Meg. "I was beginning to wonder if you were still nesting here." She had stopped breaching, but the calves continued to splash.

"YOU were wondering about ME? Meg, I've been everywhere looking for you. I was so worried," said Alice.

The good thing about a breaching whale is that it's not eating!

When a whale leaves the water in a twisting arc skyward, it is called "breaching." The reasons for this giant's acrobatics are not known for certain. It might be that humpbacks have so many reasons for breaching that they have confused their human observers. Whales breach to remove parasites, to stun prey, to show aggression or annoyance, and probably, they breach just for fun. Whatever the reason, a breaching whale is a magnificent sight.

"The twins slowed me down a bit. That's Flip on the left and Flop to the right. They like to breach and eat. We had to stop for a week in the middle of our trip to feed. Which reminds me—I'm starving," said Meg. "Let's go fishing in Wavy Kelp Bay—you know, the little bay off Big Bay, three bays up from the Loud Place, on the side where the sun rises."

"I'll meet you there," said Alice.

When they all had reached the bay, Meg showed the twins how to flick their tails and fill their mouths. In the midst of much splashing and commotion, Luty the otter popped out of the water.

"Luty!" cried Alice. "Look. It's Meg and her twins. They've come back at last! Meg, come meet Luty."

Meg surfaced just a few feet away with a mouth full of fish.

"Ah, just as I remember you Ms. Meg." smiled Luty. "Those are beautiful calves. I've made a special sculpture to celebrate your friendship with this worried little puffin. I call it 'Best Friends.'"

"Alice," said Meg. "You keep this statue at the entrance to your burrow to remind you that I will always return to you and the Supper Sea!"

Meg was calling to Alice, "Come meet Flip and Flop! They really like breaching. They just never stop.

We've come back so hungry. All summer we'll stay. Hey! Let's all go fishing in Wavy Kelp Bay."

At the Bay they met Luty, who had made a new statue. Said Meg, "Hey, that's me! And look, Alice, that's you.

"Watch me!" shouted Flop.

"No me!" shouted Flip. The bay was filled with the splashings of breaching humpback calves.

From amidst a tangle of kelp at the edge of the bay a small body lurched skyward. "No. Look at ME!" squealed Luty's pup, just before she made her own smaller, but equally splendid splash into the water.

Today Meg and Alice are still best of friends.
They fish here each summer. That's how *Meg's Song* ends.

So come way up north to the green Supper Sea
When the days are real long, it's a great place to be.

Not a bad song, but I've always preferred "Luty's Song." Less violence for the kids you know.